Lo que conozco/What I Know

CONOZCO COSAS QUE SE MUEVEN
I KNOW THINGS THAT GO

By Trisha James
Traducido por Eida de la Vega

Gareth Stevens PUBLISHING

conceptos básicos

Conozco cosas que se mueven.
Esta es una bicicleta.

I know things that go.
This is a bicycle.

Este es un monopatín.

This is a scooter.

Este es un auto.

This is a car.

Este es un camión.

This is a truck.

Este es un tractor.

This is a tractor.

Esta es una motocicleta.

This is a motorcycle.

POLICE
111
POLICE

Este es un autobús.

This is a bus.

SCHOOL BUS
STOP

Esta es una lancha.

This is a boat.

Este es un avión.

This is an airplane.

Este es un tren.

This is a train.

800
800
B&O

¿Qué forma de movilizarte prefieres?

Which way to go do you like best?

SCHOOL BUS

800

Please visit our website, www.garethstevens.com. For a free color catalog of all our high-quality books, call toll free 1-800-542-2595 or fax 1-877-542-2596.

Cataloging-in-Publication Data

Names: James, Trisha.
Title: I know things that go = Conozco cosas que se mueven / Trisha James.
Description: New York : Gareth Stevens Publishing, 2018. | Series: Lo que conozco / What I know | In English and Spanish
Identifiers: ISBN 9781538205648 (library bound)
Subjects: LCSH: Transportation–Juvenile literature. | Vehicles–Juvenile literature.
Classification: LCC TL147.J36 2017 | DDC 629.04–dc23

First Edition

Published in 2018 by
Gareth Stevens Publishing
111 East 14th Street, Suite 349
New York, NY 10003

Translator: Eida de la Vega
Editorial Director, Spanish: Nathalie Beullens-Maoui
Editor, English: Therese Shea
Designer: Sarah Liddell

Photo credits: Cover, p. 1 (stripes) Eky Studio/Shutterstock.com; cover, p. 1 (main) S_E/Shutterstock.com; pp. 3, 23 (bike) Decha Laoharuengrongkun/Shutterstock.com; p. 5 NadyaEugene/Shutterstock.com; p. 7 Peter38/Shutterstock.com; p. 9 Mike Flippo/Shutterstock.com; p. 11 Fotokostic/Shutterstock.com; p. 13 Philip Lange/Shutterstock.com; pp. 15, 23 (bus) Stuart Monk/Shutterstock.com; p. 17 Italianvideoagency/Shutterstock.com; pp. 19, 23 (airplane) IM_photo/Shutterstock.com; pp. 21, 23 (train) Kenneth Sponsler/Shutterstock.com.

Printed in the United States of America

CPSIA compliance information: Batch #CS17GS: For further information contact Gareth Stevens, New York, New York at 1-800-542-2595.